THIS BOOK IS PURELY FICTIONAL...

- BUGS DO NOT WEAR SHOES OR CARRY PURSES (UNLESS THEY ARE GOING OUT).
- BUGS DO NOT USUALLY PLAY THE DRUMS ON A SODA CAN (SOMETIMES THEY USE BOTTLE CAPS).
- THEY DO NOT PLAY TINY GUITARS OR HAVE DISCO BALLS (UNLESS IT IS A SPECIAL OCCASION).
- THEY DEFINITELY DO NOT HAVE COFFEE SHOPS INSIDE OF CRACKER BOXES OR WOOD BURNING FIREPLACES (UNLESS IT'S COLD. COFFEE AND FIREPLACES ARE A MUST IN THE WINTER.)
- GRASSHOPPERS USUALLY DON'T READ THE NEWSPAPER (THEY PREFER MAGAZINES)

THAT IS, AS FAR AS WE KNOW, BUT OF COURSE YOU CAN NEVER BE TOO SURE...

THEY LIKED TO TALK...

THEY LIKED TO EAT...

THEY LIKED PUTTING SHOES
ON THEIR LITTLE BUG FEET...

THEN ONE DAY
MAYOR ROACH ANNOUNCED
THAT A NEW BUG FAMILY
HAD COME TO TOWN

THEY WERE REALLY LONG
THEY WERE HAIRY TOO
BUT, THE BUGS OF BUGTOWN
LOVED ANYONE NEW!

THEY LOVED TO TALK...

THEY COULD REALLY EAT...

...AND THEY COULD PUT EVEN MORE SHOES ON THEIR LITTLE BUG FEET!

THEN ONE DAY
NO ONE KNEW WHY
THEIR FRIENDS DISAPPEARED
WITHOUT SAYING GOODBYE

DAYS WENT BY
THEN A WEEK CAME
BUGTOWN JUST WAS
NOT THE SAME...

NO ONE COULD TALK...

NO ONE COULD EAT...

THEY EVEN STOPPED
PUTTING SHOES ON THEIR
LITTLE BUG FEET...

THEN, SUDDENLY
THEIR FRIENDS REAPPEARED!
ALL OF BUGTOWN
DANCED AND CHEERED!

BUT, THEY DIDN'T
QUITE LOOK THE SAME
VERY DIFFERENT FROM WHEN
THEY FIRST CAME

BUGTOWN STARED
WITH GREAT SURPRISE!
NOW THEY HAD WINGS
AND THEY COULD FLY!

So, they danced and sang...

...UP TO THE SKY!

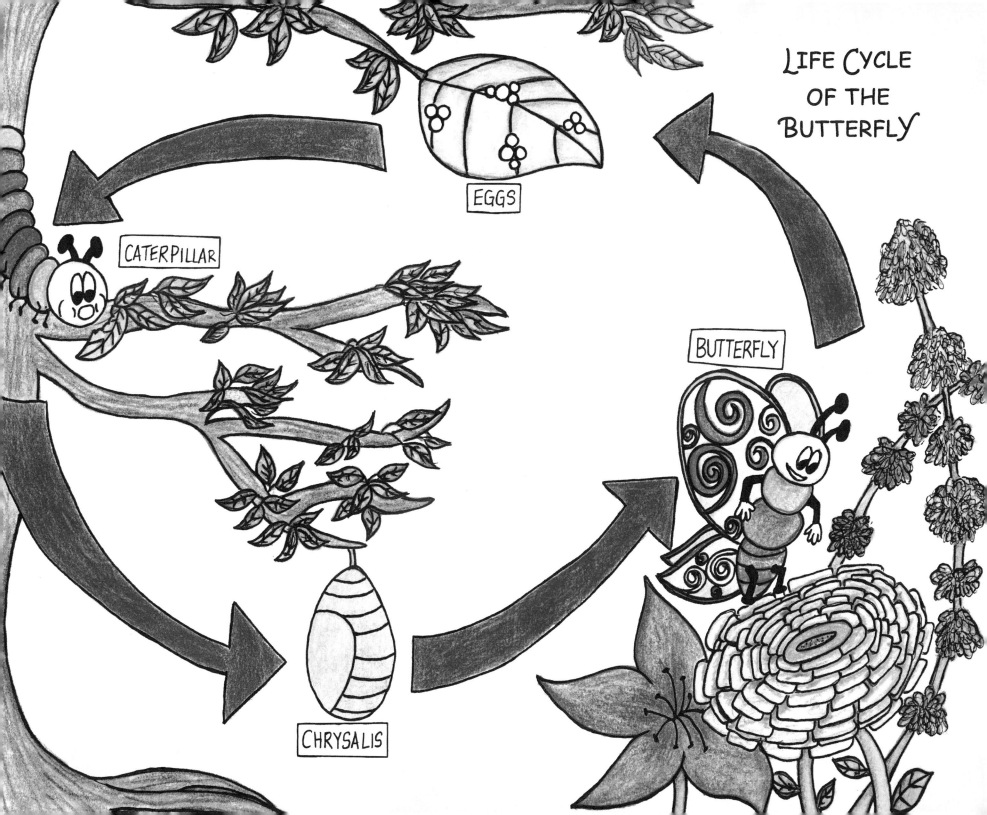

A SPECIAL THANKS TO THE RESIDENTS OF BUGTOWN FOR MAKING THIS BOOK POSSIBLE!

MS. FINLEY FLY

MRS. GAIL AND GREG GRASSHOPPER

MAYOR RYDER ROACH

MR. SHANE SPIDER

BRAYDEN BUTTERFLY

MR. FRED FLY

MRS. CAMILLE BUTTERFLY

MRS. LILY LADYBUG

MS. PEGGY PILL BUG

MR. BENTON BUTTERFLY

WALLY & WILLOW WORM

Visit

www.JuliannaWorks.com

Find out more about the author, upcoming new book releases, and to order more copies of Bugtown!

CPSIA information can be obtained
at www.ICGtesting.com
Printed in the USA
LVRC100745070722
722893LV00003B/12